This book belongs to

....

Dolly Parton

I Am a RAINBOW

Illustrated by Heather Sheffield   G. P. Putnam's Sons

I dedicate this book to all children everywhere, and to the dedicated parents and teachers who help guide and show them how to utilize their true colors.—D.P.

Dedicated with love to the memory of Myrtle Baker and Mildred Sheffield. Endless thanks as always to D.P.—a force of nature and a true friend.—H.S.

G. P. PUTNAM'S SONS

An Imprint of Penguin Random House LLC, New York

Visit us at penguinrandomhouse.com

Published simultaneously in Canada. Manufactured in China by RR Donnelley Asia Printing Solutions Ltd.

Design by Katrina Damkoehler. Text set in Heatwave. The art was created digitally.

Library of Congress Cataloging-in-Publication Data

Parton, Dolly.

I am a rainbow / Dolly Parton ; illustrated by Heather Sheffield.   p. cm.

Summary: Words and music describe different emotions in terms of color, as when everything is rosy when one feels joyful, then remind the reader that everyone experiences this same rainbow of emotions.

1. Children's songs, English–United States–Texts. [1. Emotions–Songs and music. 2. Songs.] I. Sheffield, Heather, ill. II. Title.

PZ8.3.P2714Iaac 2009   782.42–dc22   [E]   2007042834

ISBN 978-0-399-24733-0

Special Markets ISBN 978-0-399-25511-3 Not for resale

11

This Imagination Library edition is published by Penguin Young Readers, a division of Penguin Random House, exclusively for Dolly Parton's Imagination Library, a not-for-profit program designed to inspire a love of reading and learning, sponsored in part by The Dollywood Foundation. Penguin's trade editions of this work are available wherever books are sold.

When I'm tickled **PINK**,
It means I'm feeling dandy.
Everything is great and
As sweet as cotton candy.

But guess what happens when
My sister pulls my hair?
Then I turn **RED**.
I'm as angry as a bear!

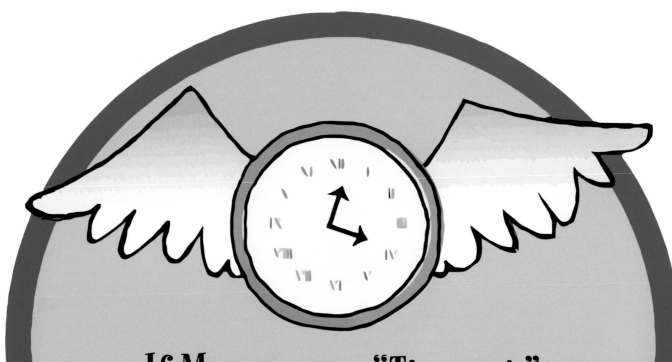

If Mommy says "Time-out,"
I pout for a minute or two.
Then I get bored and sad
And I feel kinda . . .

BLUE.

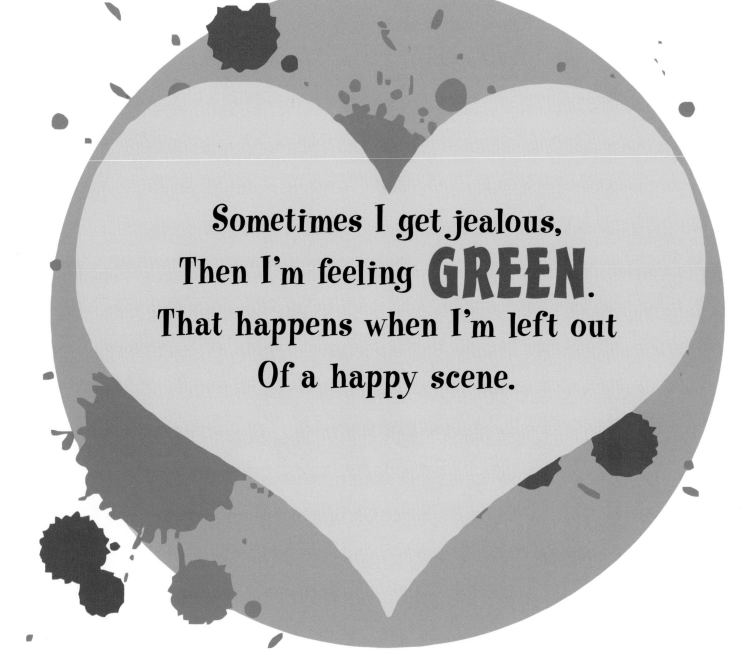

Sometimes I get jealous,
Then I'm feeling **GREEN**.
That happens when I'm left out
Of a happy scene.

When I'm feeling scared,
Kids call me YELLOW,
But I can find my courage
And be a brave fellow!

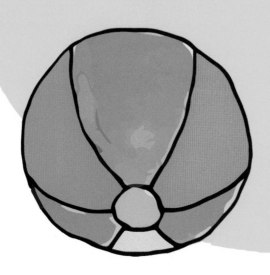

When we all play together,
It makes me feel so cozy.
My mood is joyful
And everything is ROSY.

That each and every person
Has feelings too.

It's not
always up to you,
The way that
you feel.

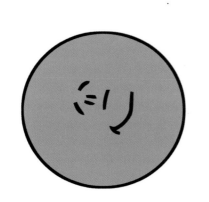
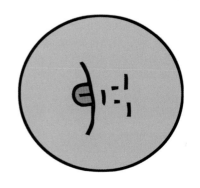

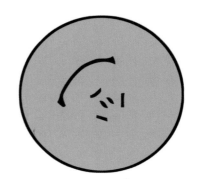

But
how you act
Is a different
deal.

So be a rainbow—
Shine above

And filter all your glow
Through love.

It's nature's way—
these colors you show.
So simply say . . .

I am a

RAINBOW!

When I was just a young child, I wanted to see a rainbow every single day. No matter how I was feeling, seeing a rainbow always made me happy. Then one day, I figured out how I could see a rainbow every day—all I had to do was reach up and pull that rainbow right out of the sky and place it in my heart.

May you all carry a rainbow in your heart so whenever you need a moment of joy, you just let that rainbow out of your heart and watch it jump back into the sky!

I love you,

Dolly